J. Hudson Taylor

A Ribband of Blue

Outlook

J. Hudson Taylor

A Ribband of Blue

1. Auflage | ISBN: 978-3-73262-706-6

Erscheinungsort: Frankfurt am Main, Deutschland

Erscheinungsjahr: 2018

Outlook Verlag GmbH, Frankfurt.

Reproduction of the original.

J. Hudson Taylor

A Ribband of Blue

Outlook

A Ribband of Blue

AND
OTHER BIBLE STUDIES

By
J. HUDSON TAYLOR.

(A companion volume to "Union and Communion,"
and to "Separation and Service.")

London
CHINA INLAND MISSION, Newington Green, N.
Morgan & Scott, 12, Paternoster Buildings, E.C.

A Ribband Of Blue.

We would draw the attention of beloved friends to the instructive passage with which the fifteenth chapter of Numbers closes; and may God, through our meditation on His precious Word, make it yet more precious and practical to each one of us, for Christ our Redeemer's sake!

The whole chapter is full of important teaching. It commences with instruction concerning the burnt-offering, the sacrifice in performing a vow, and the free-will offering. It was not to be supposed that any one might present his sacrifice to God according to his own thought and plan. If it were to be acceptable—a sweet savour unto the Lord—it must be an offering in every respect such as God had appointed. We cannot become acceptable to God in ways of our own devising; from beginning to end it must be, "Not my will, but Thine, be done."

Then, from the seventeenth to the twenty-first verse, the Lord claims a *first-fruits*. The people of God were not to eat their fill, consume all that they cared to consume, and *then* give to God somewhat of the remainder; but before they touched the bread of the land, a heave-offering was to be offered to the Lord; and when the requirement of God had been fully met, then, and not till then, were they at liberty to satisfy their own hunger and supply their own wants. How often we see the reverse of this in daily life! Not only are necessaries first supplied from the income, but every fancied luxury is procured without stint, before the question of the consecration of substance to God is really entertained.

Next follow the directions concerning errors from heedlessness and ignorance. The people were not to imagine that sin was not sinful if it were unconsciously committed. Man's knowledge and consciousness do not make wrong right or right wrong. The will of GOD was revealed and *ought* to have been known: not to know that will was in itself sinful; and not to do that will, whether consciously or unconsciously, was sin—sin that could only be put away by atoning sacrifice.

GOD dealt in much mercy and grace with those who committed sins of ignorance; though, when the sin became known and recognised, confession and sacrifice were immediately needful. But, thank GOD! the sacrifice was ordained, and the sin could be put away.

It was not so with the presumptuous sin. No sacrifice was appointed for a man, whether born in the land or a stranger, who reproached the LORD by presumptuous sin. Of that man it was said, "that soul shall utterly be cut off; his iniquity shall be upon him."

This distinction is very important to make. We are not to think that our holiest service is free from sin, or can be accepted save through JESUS CHRIST our LORD. We are not to suppose that sins of omission, any more than sins of commission, are looked lightly upon by GOD: sins of forgetfulness and heedlessness or ignorance are more than frailties—are real sins, needing atoning sacrifice. GOD deals very gently and graciously with us in these matters; when transgression or iniquity is brought home to the conscience, "if we confess our sins, He is faithful and just to forgive us our sins, and to cleanse us from all unrighteousness." Even when walking in the light, "as He is in the light," we are not beyond the need of atonement. Though our fellowship with GOD be unbroken by any conscious transgression, it continues unbroken only because "the blood of JESUS CHRIST HIS SON is cleansing us from all sin."

The man, however, who would presume on GOD's forgiveness, and despise GOD's holiness and His claim upon His people, by doing deliberately the thing that he knows to be contrary to GOD's will, that man will find spiritual dearth and spiritual death inevitably follow. His communion with GOD is brought to an end, and it is hard to say how far Satan may not be permitted to carry such a backslider in heart and life. It is awfully possible not merely to "grieve" and to "resist," but even to "quench" the SPIRIT of GOD.

We have a solemn example of presumptuous sin in the case of the man found gathering sticks on the Sabbath day. He was not—he could not be ignorant of GOD'S ordinance concerning the Sabbath. The gathering of sticks was not to meet a necessity; his case was not parallel with that of the poor man who perhaps had received his wages late on Saturday night, and has had no opportunity of purchasing food in time to prepare it for the day of rest. To the Israelite, the double supply of manna was given on the morning of the day before the Sabbath; and as the uncooked manna would not keep, it was necessary that early in that day it should be prepared for food. He had, therefore, no need of sticks to cook his Sabbath's dinner. And the country was so hot that no man would kindle a fire from choice or preference. His object in gathering sticks was simply to show, openly and publicly, that he despised God, and refused to obey His holy ordinance: rightly, therefore, was that man put to death.

But occasion was taken in connection with this judgment to introduce the wearing of the

"RIBBAND OF BLUE."

God would have all His people wear a badge. Throughout their generations they were to make them fringes in the borders of their garments, and to put upon the fringe of the borders a ribband of blue, that they might look upon it and remember all the commandments of the Lord, and do them, and might be a holy people, holy unto their God, who brought them out of the land of Egypt, to be their God.

Blue is the colour of heaven. The beautiful waters of the sea reflect it, and are as blue as the cloudless sky. When the clouds come between, then, and then only, is the deep blue lost. But it is the will of God that there should never be a cloud between His people and Himself; and that, as the Israelite of old, wherever he went, carried the ribband of blue, so His people to-day should manifest a heavenly spirit and temper wherever they go; and should, like Moses, in their very countenances bear witness to the glory and beauty of the God whom they love and serve.

How interesting it must have been to see that ribband of blue carried by the farmer into the field, by the merchant to his place of business, by the maid-servant into the innermost parts of the dwelling, when performing her daily duties. Is it less important that the Christian of today, called to be a witness for Christ, should be manifestly characterised by His spirit? Should we not all be "imitators of God, as dear children," and "walk in love as Christ also hath loved us, and hath given Himself for us"? And should not this Spirit of God-likeness be carried into the smallest details of life, and not be merely reserved for special occasions? If we understand aright the meaning of our Saviour's direction "Be ye therefore perfect, even as your Father which is in heaven is perfect," it teaches this great truth.

We are to be the salt of the earth and the light of the world, not to break one of the least of the commandments, not to give way to anger, not to tolerate the thought of impurity, to give no rash promises, or in conversation to say more than yea or nay. The spirit of retaliation is not to be indulged in; a yieldingness of spirit is to characterise the child of the kingdom; those who hate and despitefully use us are to be pitied, and loved, and prayed for. Then comes the direction, "Be ye therefore perfect, even as your F<small>ATHER</small> which is in heaven is perfect." In the little frictions of daily life, as well as in the more serious trials and persecutions to which the Christian is exposed, he is to be manifestly an imitator of his heavenly F<small>ATHER</small>.

Now, G<small>OD'S</small> perfection is an absolute perfection; while ours, at best, is only relative. A needle may be a perfect needle, in every respect adapted for the work for which it was made. It is not, however, a microscopic object; under magnifying power it becomes a rough, honeycombed poker, with a ragged hole in the place of the eye. But it was not made to be a microscopic object; and, being adapted to the purpose for which it was made, it may properly be considered a perfect needle. So we are not called to be perfect angels, or in any respect Divine, but we are called to be perfect Christians, performing the privileged duties that as such devolve upon us.

Our F<small>ATHER</small> makes *according to His perfection* the least little thing that He makes. The tiniest fly, the smallest animalcule, the dust of a butterfly's wing, however highly you may magnify them, are seen to be absolutely perfect. Should not the little things of our daily life be as relatively perfect in the case of each Christian as the lesser creations of G<small>OD</small> are absolutely perfect? Ought we not to glorify G<small>OD</small> in the formation of each letter that we write, and as Christians to write a more legible hand than unconverted people can be expected to do? Ought we not to be more thorough in our service, not simply doing well that which will be seen and noticed, but as our F<small>ATHER</small> makes many a flower to bloom unseen in the lonely desert, so to do all that we can do, as under His eye, though no other eye ever take note of it?

It is our privilege to take our rest and recreation for the purpose of pleasing Him; to lay aside our garments at night neatly (for He is in the room, and watches over us while we sleep), to wash, to dress, to smooth the hair, with His eye in view; and, in short, in all that we are and in all that we do to use the full measure of ability which G<small>OD</small> has given us to the glory of His holy Name? Were we always so to live, how beautiful Christian life would become! how much more worthy a witness we should bear to the world of Him whose witnesses we are! May the life we are living be characterised by the growth in grace which will glorify G<small>OD</small>; and may tell-tale faces, and glad hearts, and loving service be to each one of us as "a ribband of blue," reflecting the very hue of heaven, and reminding ourselves and one another of our privileges to "remember all the commandments of the L<small>ORD</small>, and do them."

Blessed Prosperity

Meditations On The First Psalm.

INTRODUCTORY.

There is a prosperity which is not blessed: it comes not from above but from beneath, and it leads away from, not towards heaven. This prosperity of the wicked is often a sore perplexity to the servants of God; they need to be reminded of the exhortation, "Fret not thyself because of him who prospereth in his way, because of the man who bringeth wicked devices to pass." Many besides the Psalmist have been envious at the foolish when seeing the prosperity of the wicked, and have been tempted to ask, "Is there knowledge in the Most High?" While Satan remains the God of this world, and has it is his power to prosper his votaries, this source of perplexity will always continue to those who do not enter into the sanctuary and consider the latter end of the worldling.

Nor is it the godless only who are tempted by the offer of a prosperity which comes from beneath. Our Saviour Himself was tempted by the arch-enemy in this way. Christ was told that all that He desired to accomplish for the kingdoms of this world might be effected by an easier path than the cross—a little compromise with him who held the power and was able to bestow the kingdoms, and all should be His own. The lying wiles of the seducer were instantly rejected by our Lord; not so ineffective are such wiles to many of His people; a little policy rather than the course for which conscience pleads; a little want of integrity in business dealings; a little compromise with the ways of the world, followed by a prosperity which brings no blessing, these prove often that the enemy's arts are still the same.

But, thank God! There is a true prosperity which comes from Him and leads towards Him. It is not only consistent with perfect integrity and uncompromising holiness of heart and life, but it cannot be attained without them, and its enjoyment tends to deepen them. This divine prosperity is God's purpose for every believer, in *all* that he undertakes; in things temporal and in things spiritual, in all the relations and affairs of this life, as well as in all work for Christ and for eternity, it is God's will for each child of His that *"whatsoever he doeth shall prosper."*

Yet many of His children evidently do not enjoy this uniform blessing; some find failure rather than success the rule of their life: while others, sometimes prospered and sometimes discouraged, live lives of uncertainty, in which anxiety and even fear are not infrequent. Shall we not each one at the outset ask, How is it with me? Is this blessed prosperity my experience? Am I so led by the S*pirit* in my doings, and so prospered by G*od* in their issues, that as His witness I can bear testimony to His faithfulness to this promise? If it be not so with me, what is the reason? Which of the necessary conditions have I failed to fulfil? May our meditations on the First Psalm make these conditions more clear to our minds, and may faith be enabled to claim definitely all that is included in this wonderful promise!

THE NEGATIVE CONDITIONS OF BLESSING

"Blessed is the man that walketh not in the counsel of the ungodly."

More literally, O the blessings, the manifold happiness of the man whose character is here described in the first and second verses of this Psalm! He is happy in what he escapes or avoids, and happy and prospered in what he undertakes.

The first characteristic given us is that he walks not in the counsel of the ungodly, the wicked. Notice, it does not merely say that he walks not in wicked counsel: a man of G*od* clearly would not do this; but what is said is that he "walketh not in the counsel of the wicked." Now the wicked have often much worldly wisdom, and become noted for their prosperity and their prudence, but the child of G*od* should always be on his guard against *their* counsel; however good it may appear, it is full of danger.

One of the principal characteristics of the wicked is that G*od* is not in all his thoughts; he sees everything from the standpoint of self, or, at the highest, from the standpoint of humanity. His maxim, "Take care of number one," would be very good if it were meant that G*od* is first, and should always be put first; but he means it not so: self and not G*od* is number one to the ungodly. The wicked will often counsel to honesty, not on the ground that honesty is pleasing to G*od*, but that it is the best policy; if in any particular business transaction a more profitable policy appears quite safe, those who have simply been honest because it pays best, will be very apt to cease to be so.

The child of G*od* has no need of the counsel of the ungodly; if he love and study G*od*'s Word it will make him wiser than all such counsellors. If he seek for and observe all the counsel of G*od*, through the guidance of the H*oly* S*pirit*, he will not walk in darkness even as to worldly things. The directions of G*od*'s Word may often seem strange and impolitic, but in the measure in which he has faith to obey the directions he finds in the Scripture, turning not to the right hand nor to the left, will he make his way prosperous, will he find good success.

The history of the early Friends in America, who would not take a weapon to protect themselves against the savage Indian tribes, shows how safe it is to follow the Word of God and not to resist evil. And their later experience in the recent Civil War, in which no one of them lost his life, though exposed to the greatest dangers and hardships because they would not fight, further confirms the wisdom as well as blessedness of literally obeying the Scripture. The eyes of the Lord still run to and fro throughout the whole earth to show Himself strong in behalf of those who put their trust in Him before the sons of men. The enlightened believer has so much better counsel that he no more needs than condescends to accept the counsel of the ungodly.

And, more than this, the wise child of God will carefully ascertain the standpoint of a fellow-believer before he will value his counsel; for he learns from Scripture and experience that Satan too infrequently makes handles of the people of God, as, for instance, in Peter's case. Little did the astonished Peter know whence his exhortation to the Lord to pity Himself came; "Get thee behind me, Satan," showed that our Lord had traced this counsel, which did not seek first the Kingdom of God, to its true source. Alas, the counsel of worldly-minded Christians does far more harm than that of the openly wicked. Whenever the supposed interests of self, or family, or country, or even of church or mission come first, we may be quite sure of the true source of that counsel; it is at least earthly or sensual, if not devilish.

Further, the truly blessed man—

Standeth not in the way of sinners.

Birds of a feather flock together; the way of a sinner no more suits a true believer than the way of the believer suits the sinner. As a witness for his Master in the hope of saving the lost, he may go to them; but he will not, like Lot, pitch his tent towards Sodom; lest he be ensnared as Lot was, who only escaped himself, losing all those he loved best, and all his possessions. Ah, how many parents who have fluttered moth-like near the flame, have seen their children destroyed by it, while they themselves have not escaped unscathed! How many churches and Christian institutions, in the attempt to attract the unconverted by worldly inducements or amusements, have themselves forfeited the blessing of God; and have so lost spiritual power, that those whom they have thus attracted have been nothing benefited! Instead of seeing the dead quickened, a state of torpor and death has crept over themselves.

There is no need of, nor room for, any other attraction than that which Christ Himself gave, when He said, "I, if I be lifted up … will draw all men unto

Me." Our MASTER was ever "separate from sinners," and the HOLY SPIRIT speaks unmistakably in 2 Cor. vi.: "What fellowship hath righteousness with unrighteousness? And what communion hath light with darkness? ... for ye are the temple of the living GOD; as GOD hath said, I will dwell in them, and walk in them; and I will be their GOD, and they shall be my people. Wherefore come out from among them, and be ye separate ... and touch not the unclean thing; and I will receive you, and will be a FATHER unto you, and ye shall be my sons and daughters, saith the LORD Almighty."

"Nor sitteth in the seat of the scornful."

The seat of the scornful is one of the special dangers of this age. Pride, presumption, and scorn are closely linked together, and are far indeed from the mind which was in CHRIST JESUS. This spirit often shows itself in the present day in the form of irreverent criticism. Those who are spiritually least qualified for it are to be found sitting in the seat of judgment, rather than taking the place of the inquirer and the learner. The Bereans of old did not scornfully reject the, to them, strange teachings of the Apostle Paul, but searched the Scriptures daily to see whether these things were so. Now, forsooth, the Scriptures themselves are called in question, and the very foundations of Christian faith are abandoned by men who would fain be looked upon as the apostles of modern thought. May GOD preserve His people from abandoning the faith once for all delivered to the saints, for the baseless ephemeral fancies of the present day!

THE POSITIVE CONDITIONS OF BLESSING.

We have considered the things which are avoided by the truly blessed man. O, the miseries and the losses of those who fail to avoid them! We have now to dwell upon the special characteristics of the man of GOD, those which are at once the source of his strength and his shield of protection.

"His delight is in the law of the LORD;
"And in His law doth he meditate day and night."

The unregenerate *cannot* delight in the law of the LORD. They may be very religious, and may read the Bible as one of their religious duties. They may admire much that is in the Bible, and be loud in its praise—for as a mere book it is the most wonderful in the world. Nay, they may go much further than this; and may imagine, as did Saul the persecutor, that their life is ordered by its teachings, while still they are far from GOD. But when such become converted, they discover they have been blind; among the "all things" that become new, they find that they have got a new Bible; and as new-born babes they desire the unadulterated milk of the Word that they may grow thereby. Well is it when young Christians are properly fed from the Word of God, and have not their taste corrupted, and their spiritual constitution destroyed, by feeding on the imaginations of men rather than on the verities of God.

It is not difficult to discover what a man delights in. "Out of the abundance of the heart the mouth speaketh." The mother delights to speak of her babe, the politician loves to talk of politics, the scientific man of his favourite science, and the athlete of his sport. In the same way the earnest, happy Christian manifests his delight in the Word of God; it is his food and comfort; it is his study and his guide; and as the Holy Spirit throws fresh light on its precious truths he finds in it a joy and pleasure beyond compare. Naturally and spontaneously he will often speak of that which is so precious to his heart.

By regeneration the believer, having become the *child* of God, finds new interest and instruction in all the works of God. His FATHER designed and created them, upholds and uses them, and for His glory they exist. But this is peculiarly true of the Word of God. Possessing the mind of CHRIST, instructed by the SPIRIT of CHRIST, he finds in every part of God's Word testimony to the person and work of his adorable Master and Friend. The Bible in a thousand ways endears itself to him, while unfolding the mind and ways of God, His past dealing with His people, and His wonderful revelations of the future.

While thus studying God's Word the believer becomes conscious of a new source of delight; not only is that which is revealed precious, but the beauty and perfection of the revelation itself grows upon him. He has now no need of external evidence to prove its inspiration; it everywhere bears the impress of Divinity. And as the microscope which reveals the coarseness and blemishes of the works of man only shows more fully the perfectness of God's works, and brings to light new and unimagined beauties, so it is with the Word of God when closely scanned.

In what remarkable contrast does this Book stand to the works of men! The science of yesterday is worthless to-day; but history and the discoveries of our own times only confirm the reliability of these ancient sacred records. The stronger our faith in the plenary, verbal inspiration of God's Holy Word, the more fully we make it our guide, and the more implicitly we follow its teachings, the deeper will be our peace and the more fruitful our service. "Great peace have they which love Thy law: and nothing shall offend them." Becoming more and more convinced of the divine wisdom of the directions and commands of Scripture, and of the reliability of the promises, the life of the believer will become increasingly one of obedience and trust; and thus he will prove for himself how good, acceptable, and perfect is the will of God, and that Bible which reveals it.

The words, "the Law of the Lord," which we understand to mean the whole Word of God, are very suggestive. They indicate that the Bible is intended to teach us what God would have us to *do;* that we should not merely seek for the promises, and try to get all we can from God; but should much more earnestly desire to know what he wants us *to be* and *to do* for Him. It is recorded of Ezra, that he prepared his heart to *seek* the Law of the Lord, in order that he might *do* it, and *teach* in Israel the statutes and judgments. The result was that the hand of his God was upon him for good, the desires of his heart were largely granted, and he became the channel of blessing to his whole people. Every one who searches the Scriptures in the same spirit will receive and communicate the blessing of God: he will find in it the guidance he needs for his own service, and oft-times a word in season for those with whom he is associated.

But not only will the Bible become the Law of the Lord to him as teaching and illustrating what God would have him to be and to do, but still more as revealing what God Himself is and does. As the law of gravitation gives us to know how a power, on which we may ever depend, will act under given circumstances, so the Law of the Lord gives us to know Him, and the principles of His government, on which we may rely with implicit confidence.

The man of God will also delight to trace God in the Word as the great Worker, and rejoice in the privilege of being a fellow-worker with Him—a glad, voluntary agent in doing the will of God, yet rejoicing in the grace that has made him willing, and in the mighty, divine power that works through him. The Bible will also teach him to view himself as but an atom, as it were, in God's great universe; and to see God's great work as a magnificent whole, carried on by ten thousand agencies; carried on through all spheres, in all time, and without possibility of ultimate failure—a glorious manifestation of the perfections of the great Worker! He himself, and a thousand more of his fellow-servants, may pass away; but this thought will not paralyse his efforts, for he knows that whatever has been wrought in God will abide, and that whatever is incomplete when his work is done the great Worker will in His own time and way bring to completion.

He does not expect to understand all about the grand work in which he is privileged to take a blessed but infinitesimal part; he can afford to await its completion, and can already by faith rejoice in the certainty that the whole will be found in every respect worthy of the great Designer and Executor. Well may his delight be in the Law of the Lord, and well may he meditate in it day and night.

THE OUTCOME IN BLESSING.

We next proceed to notice the remarkable promises in the third verse of this Psalm—one of the most remarkable and inclusive contained in the Scriptures:

"And he shall be like a tree planted by the rivers of water,
"That bringeth forth his fruit in his season;
"His leaf also shall not wither;
"And whatsoever he doeth shall prosper."

If we could offer to the ungodly a worldly plan which would ensure their prospering in all that they undertake, how eagerly they would embrace it! And yet when G‍od Himself reveals an effectual plan to His people how few avail themselves of it! Many fail on the negative side and do not come clearly out of the world; many fail on the positive side and allow other duties or indulgences to take the time that should be given to reading and meditation on G‍od's Word. To some it is not at all easy to secure time for the morning watch, but nothing can make up for the loss of it. But is there not yet a third class of Christians whose failure lies largely in their not embracing the promise and claiming it by faith? In each of these three ways failure may come in and covenant blessings may be lost.

Let us now consider what are the blessings, the manifold happinesses which faith is to claim when the conditions are fulfilled.

I. *Stability.*—He shall be like a tree (not a mere annual plant), of steady progressive growth and increasing fruitfulness. A tree planted, and always to be found in its place, not blown about, the sport of circumstances. The flowers may bloom and pass away, but the tree abides.

II. *Independent Supplies.*—Planted by the rivers of water. The ordinary supplies of rain and dew may fail: his deep and hidden supplies cannot. He shall not be careful in the year of drought, and in the days of famine he shall be satisfied. His supply is the living water—the S‍pirit of G‍od—the same yesterday, today, and forever: hence he depends on no intermitting spring.

III. *Seasonable Fruitfulness.*—The careful student of Scripture will notice the parallelism between the teaching of the First Psalm and that of our L‍ord in the Gospel of John, where in the sixth chapter we are taught that he who feeds on C‍hrist abides in Him, and in the fifteenth that he who abides brings forth much fruit. We feed upon C‍hrist the incarnate W‍ord through the written Word. So in this Psalm he who delights in the Law of the L‍ord, and meditates upon it day and night, brings forth his fruit in his season.

There is something beautiful in this. A word spoken in season how good it is; how even a seasonable look will encourage or restrain, reprove or comfort! The promise reminds one of those in John about the living water thirsty ones drink, and are not only refreshed, but become channels through which rivers of living water are always flowing, so that other thirsty ones in their hour of need may find seasonable refreshment. But the figure in the Psalm is not that of water flowing through us as through a channel; but that of fruit, the very outcome of our own transformed life—a life of union with C̶ʜ̶ʀ̶ɪ̶s̶ᴛ̶.

It is so gracious of our Gᴏᴅ not to work through us in a mere mechanical way, but to make us branches of the True Vine, the very organs by which Its fruit is produced. We are not, therefore, independent workers, for there is a fundamental difference between fruit and work. Work is the outcome of effort; fruit, of life. A bad man may do good work, but a bad tree cannot bear good fruit. The result of work is not reproductive, but fruit has its seed in itself. The workman has to seek his material and his tools, and often to set himself with painful perseverance to his task. The fruit of the Vine is the glad, free, spontaneous outcome of the life within; and it forms and grows and ripens in its proper season.

And what is the fruit which the believer should bear? May it not be expressed by one word—Christliness? It is interesting to notice that the Scripture does not speak of *the fruits* of the Sᴘɪʀɪᴛ, in the plural, as though we might take our choice among the graces named, but of *the fruit*, in the singular, which is a rich cluster composed of love, joy, peace, longsuffering, etc. How blessed to bring forth such fruit in its season!

IV. *Continuous Vigour.*—"His leaf also shall not wither." In our own climate many trees are able to maintain their life throughout the winter, but unable to retain their leaves. The hardy evergreen, however, not only lives, but manifests its life, and all the more conspicuously because of the naked branches around. The life within is too strong to fear the shortened day, the cold blast, or the falling snow. So with the man of Gᴏᴅ whose life is maintained by hidden communion through the Word; adversity only brings out the strength and the reality of the life within.

The leaf of the tree is no mere adornment. If the root suggests to us receptive power in that it draws from the soil the stimulating sap, without which life could not be maintained, the leaves no less remind us of the grace of giving, and of purifying. They impart to the atmosphere a grateful moisture; they provide for the traveller a refreshing shade, and they purify the air poisoned by the breathings of animal life.

Well, too, is the tree repaid for all that it gives out through its leaves. The thin stimulating sap that comes from the root, which could not of itself build up the tree, thickens in giving out its moisture, and through the leaves possesses itself of carbon from the atmosphere. Thus enriched, the sap goes back through the tree, building it up until the tiniest rootlets are as much nourished by the leaves as the latter are fed by the roots. Keep a tree despoiled of its leaves sufficiently long and it will surely die. So unless the believer is giving as well as receiving, purifying his life and influence, he cannot grow nor properly maintain his own vitality. But he who delights in the Law of the Lord, and meditates in it day and night—his leaf shall *not* wither.

V. *Uniform Prosperity.*—"Whatsoever he doeth shall prosper." Could any promise go beyond this? It is the privilege of the child of God to see the hand of God in all his circumstances and surroundings, and to serve God in all his avocations and duties. Whether he eat or drink, work or rest, speak or be silent; in all his occupations, spiritual, domestic, or secular, he is alike the servant of God. Nothing lawful to him is too small to afford an opportunity of glorifying God; duties in themselves trivial or wearisome become exalted and glorified when the believer recognises his power through them to gladden and satisfy the loving heart of his ever-observant Master. And he who in all things recognises himself as the servant *of* God may count on a sufficiency *from* God for all manner of need, and look with confident expectation *to* God to *really* prosper him in whatever he does.

But this prosperity will not always be apparent, except to the eye of faith. When Chorazin and Bethsaida rejected our Lord's message, it needed the eye of faith to rejoice in spirit and say, "Even so, Father; for so it seemed good in Thy sight." Doubtless the legions of hell rejoiced when they saw the Lord of Glory nailed to the accursed tree; yet we know that never was our blessed Lord more prospered than when, as our High Priest, He offered Himself as our atoning sacrifice, and bore our sins in His own body on the tree. As then, so now, the path of real prosperity will often lie through deepest suffering; followers of Christ may well be content with the path which He trod.

But though this prosperity may not be immediately apparent, it will always be real, and should always be claimed by faith. The minister in his church, the missionary among the heathen, the merchant at his desk, the mother in her home, the workman in his labour, each may alike claim it. Not in vain is it written, "Whatsoever he doeth shall prosper."

VI. Finally, let us notice that these promises are all in the indicative mood, and, provided the conditions are fulfilled, are absolute. There is no "may be" about them. And further, they are made to individual believers. If other believers fail, he who accepts them will not; the word is, "Whatsoever he doeth shall prosper."

THE CONTRAST.

"The ungodly are not so."

It is not necessary to dwell at any length upon the contrast. The ungodly cannot enjoy the happiness of the child of GOD, for they cannot carry out the conditions. They neither can, nor desire to, avoid the counsel, the society, or the ways of their own fellows; and they lack that spiritual insight which is essential to delighting in GOD'S Word. Instead of being full of life, like the tender grain, they become hard and dry; and the same sun that ripens the one prepares the other for destruction. Instead of being "planted," the wind drives them away; and He who delights in the way of His people, causes the way of the ungodly to perish.

Blessed Adversity.

INTRODUCTORY.

In our meditations on the first Psalm we have dwelt on "Blessed Prosperity." But all GOD'S dealings are full of blessing: He *is* good, and doeth good, good only, and continually. The believer who has taken the LORD as his SHEPERD, can assuredly say in the words of the twenty-third Psalm, "Surely goodness and mercy shall follow me all the days of my life, and I will dwell in the house of the LORD for ever;" or, taking the marginal reading of the Revised Version, "Only goodness and mercy shall follow me." Hence, we may be sure that days of adversity are still days of prosperity aso, and are full of blessing.

The believer does not need to wait until he sees the reason of GOD'S afflictive dealings with him ere he is satisfied; he *knows* that all things work together for good to them that love GOD; that all GOD'S dealings are those of a loving FATHER, who only permits that which for the time being is grievous, in order the accomplish results that cannot be achieved in any less painful way. The wise and trustful child of GOD rejoices in tribulation, "knowing that tribulation worketh patience," experience, hope—a hope that "maketh not ashamed; because the love of GOD is shed abroad in our hearts by the HOLY GHOST which is given unto us."

The history of Job is full of instruction, and should teach us many lessons of deep interest and great profit. The veil is taken away from the unseen world, and we learn much of the power of our great adversary; but also of his powerlessness apart from the permission of GOD our FATHER.

GOD'S TESTIMONY AND CHALLENGE.

"The LORD gave, and the LORD hath taken away; blessed be the Name of the

Lord."—Job i.21.

In the 8th verse of the 1st chapter, God Himself bears testimony to His servant: "that there is none like him in the earth, a perfect and an upright man, one that feareth God, and escheweth evil; and in the 2nd chapter and 3rd verse, He repeats the same testimony, adding: "still he holdeth fast his integrity, although thou movedst Me against him, to destroy him without cause." Stronger testimony to the life which God's grace enabled Job to live can scarcely be imagined. The chastisement that came upon him is declared to have been without cause so far as his life and spirit were concerned. Let us thank God that the same grace which enabled Job, so long ago, to live a life that pleased God and received His repeated commendation, is unchanged; and that by it we may also live lives that will be well-pleasing to Him with whom we have to do.

Satan would very frequently harass the believer in times of sorrow and trial by leading him to think that God is angry with him—that this is a punishment for some unknown offence, and many of the comforts and consolations that might otherwise be enjoyed may thus be clouded. Do we not rather see from the Word of God that He is like a glad father, delighting to be able to encourage a strong healthy son to undertake some athletic feat which will entail arduous effort and careful training, or to stimulate him to prepare for a difficult literary examination by a prolonged and toilsome course of study, knowing he will obtain honours and permanent advantage from his attainments? So, our Heavenly FATHER delights *to trust a trustworthy child with a trial* in which he can bring great glory to God, and through which he will receive permanent enlargement of heart, and blessing for himself and others.

Take the case of Abraham: God so thoroughly trust him, that He was not afraid to call upon His servant to offer up his well-beloved son. And here, in the case of Job, it was not Satan who challenged God about Job, but God who challenged the arch-enemy, the accuser of the brethren, to find any flaw in his character, or failure in his life. In each case grace triumphed, and in each case patience and fidelity were abundantly rewarded; but more of this anon.

The reply of Satan is noteworthy. He does not need to ask, "Which Job?" or, "Where does he live?" He *had* considered God's servant, and evidently knew all about him. How came it that he was so well acquainted with this faithful man of God? It may have come about in this way: those subordinate spirits of evil who are evidently under the control of Satan had in vain tried ordinary means of temptation with the patriarch. Probably reporting their want of success to some of the principalities and powers of evil, these likewise had essayed their diabolical arts, but had not succeeded in leading Job to swerve from his integrity. Last of all, the great arch-enemy himself had found all his own efforts ineffectual to harass and lead astray God's beloved servant. He found a hedge around him, and about his servants, and about his house, and about all that he had on every side—an entrenchment so strong that he had been unable to break through, so high that, going about as a roaring lion, he had been unable to leap over, or to bring disaster within the God-protected circle.

How blessed it must have been to dwell so protected! The work of Job's hands was prospered—his substance increased in the land, and he became the greatest as well as the best of all the men of the East, for in that day God manifested His approval largely, though not solely, by the bestowal of temporal blessings.

Is there no analogous spiritual blessing to be enjoyed now-a-days? Thank God, there is. Every believer may be as safely kept and as fully blessed, though, perhaps, not in the same way, as Job—may be delivered from the power of the enemy, and preserved in a charmed circle of perfect peace. The conditions are simple, and are given us by the Apostle Paul in the 4th chapter of Philippians, v. 4-7, "Rejoice in the Lord always ... Let your moderation [your gentleness, or yieldingness] be known unto all men. The Lord is at hand." Not your power of resistance of evil, and of "maintaining your own rights;" but your spirit of yieldingness, believing that the Lord will maintain for you all that is really for your good; and that in any case, He is at hand, and will soon abundantly reward fidelity to His command. And lastly, "Be careful for nothing; but in everything by prayer and supplication with thanksgiving let your requests be made known unto God. And the peace of God, which passeth all understanding, shall keep your hearts and minds through Christ Jesus."

How is it that believers so often fail to enjoy this promised blessing? Is it not that we fail to be anxious for *nothing*, and to bring *everything* by prayer and supplication with thanksgiving before God? We may bring nine difficulties out of ten to Him, and try to manage the tenth ourselves, and that one little difficulty, like a small leak that runs the vessel dry, is fatal to the whole; like a small breach in a city wall, it gives entrance to the power of the foe. But if we fulfil the conditions, He is certainly faithful, and instead of our having to keep our hearts and minds—our affections and thoughts—we shall find them kept for us. The peace, which we can neither make nor keep, will itself, as a garrison, keep and protect us, and the cares and worries will strive to enter in vain.

THE TESTING OF JOB

Reverting to the history of Job: the great accuser, having no fault to find with his character or life, insinuates that it is all the result of selfishness. "Doth Job fear G<small>OD</small> for nought." Indeed, he did not, as Satan well knew! Nor has anyone, before or since, ever feared G<small>OD</small> for nought. There is no service which pays so well as the service of our H<small>EAVENLY</small> M<small>ASTER</small>; there is none so royally rewarded. Satan was making a true assertion, but the insinuation he connected with it, that it was for the *sake* of this reward that Job served G<small>OD</small>, was not true.

To vindicate the character of Job himself in the sight of the angels of G<small>OD</small>, as well as of the evil spirits, Satan is permitted to test Job, and take away all those treasures for the sake of which alone Satan imagined, or pretended to imagine, that Job was serving G<small>OD</small>. "All that he hath," said G<small>OD</small>, "is in thy power; only upon himself put not forth thine hand."

SATAN'S MALIGNITY.

And soon Satan showed the malignity of his character by bringing disaster after disaster upon the devoted man. By his emissaries he incited the Sabeans, and they fell upon the oxen and the asses feeding beside them, slaying the servants with the edge of the sword, suffering one only to escape—and this, not in any pity or sympathy, but that he might bear the message to his unhappy master, telling of the destruction of his property and servants. The evil one appears, also, to have had power to bring the lightning from heaven
—by which the sheep, and the servants caring for them, were destroyed. Here, again, one servant only was left, by his message to increase the distress of the afflicted man of G<small>OD</small>.

Working in another direction, the Chaldeans were led to come in three bands and carry off Job's camels, slaying all the servants with the edge of the sword, save the one left to convey the evil tidings. And, as if this were not sufficient, even the very children of Job, his seven sons and three daughters—children of so many prayers—were swept away at one blow, by a terrible hurricane from the wilderness, which smote the four corners of the house so that it fell upon them, leaving only one servant to bear witness of the calamity. One only of all his family—his wife—seems to have been left to Job. But so far from being a spiritual help to him in this hour of sorrow and trial, she lost faith in GOD; and when further calamity came upon him, and he was in sore bodily suffering and affliction, his trial was added to by the words of his despairing wife: "Curse GOD, and die." We see from this, that even she was left to Job through no mercy on the part of the great enemy, but simply to fill the cup of affliction to the full in the hour of his extremity.

GRACE SUFFICIENT.

But He who sent the trial gave also the needful grace, and in the words which we have already quoted, Job replied: "The LORD gave, and the LORD hath taken away; blessed be the Name of the LORD."

Was not Job mistaken? Should he not have said: "The LORD gave, and Satan hath taken away?" No, there was no mistake. The same grace which had enabled him unharmed to receive blessing from the hand of GOD, enabled him also to discern the hand of GOD in the calamities which had befallen him. Even Satan himself did not presume to ask of GOD to be allowed *himself* to afflict Job. In the 1st chapter and the 11th verse he says: "Put forth *Thine* hand now, and touch all that he hath, and he will curse Thee to Thy face;" and in the 2nd chapter and the 5th verse: "Put forth *Thine* hand now, and touch his bone and his flesh, and he will curse Thee to Thy face." Satan knew that *none but* GOD could touch Job; and when Satan was permitted to afflict him, Job was quite right in recognising the LORD Himself as the doer of these things which He permitted to be done.

Oftentimes shall we be helped and blessed if we bear this in mind—that Satan is *servant*, and not *master*, and that he, and wicked men incited by him are only permitted to do that which GOD by His determinate counsel and foreknowledge has before determined shall be done. Come joy, or come sorrow, we may always take it from the hand of GOD.

Judas betrayed his Master with a kiss. Our LORD did not stop short at Judas, not did He even stop at the great enemy who filled the heart of Judas to do this thing; but He said: "the cup which *My FATHER* hath given me, shall I not drink it?" How the tendency to resentment and a wrong feeling would be removed, could we take an injury from the hand of a loving FATHER, instead of looking chiefly at the agent through whom it comes to us! It matters not who is the postman—it is with the writer of the letter that we are concerned: it matters not who is the messenger—it is with GOD that His children have to do.

We conclude, therefore, that Job was *not* mistaken, and that *we* shall not be mistaken if we follow his example, in accepting all GOD'S providential dealings, as from Himself. We may be sure that they will issue in ultimate blessing; because GOD is GOD, and, therefore, "all things work together for good" to them that love Him.

DEEPER TRIALS.

Job's trial, however, was not completed, as we have seen, when his property was removed. When the LORD challenged Satan a second time: "Hast thou considered my servant Job ... ?" Satan has no word of commendation, but a further insinuation: "Skin for skin, yea, all that a man hath will he give for his life ... touch his bone and his flesh, and he will curse Thee to Thy face." Receiving further permission to afflict him bodily, but with the charge withal to save his life, Satan went forth from the presence of the LORD, and smote Job with sore boils from the sole of his foot to his crown.

The pain of his disease, the loathsomeness of his appearance, must have been very great; when his friends came to see him they knew him not. His skin was broken and had become loathsome; his flesh was clothed with worms and clods of dust. Days of vanity and wearisome nights followed in sad succession; his rest at night was scared by dreams and terrified through visions; so that, without ease or respite, strangling would have been a relief to him, and death chosen rather than life. But of death there was no danger, for Satan had been charged not to touch his life.

His kinsfolk failed him, and his familiar friends seem to have forgotten him. Those who dwelt in his house counted him as a stranger, and his servant gave no answer to his call when he entreated help from him. Nay, worse than all, his own wife turned from him, and in his grief he exclaimed: "My breath is strange to my wife, though I entreated for the children's sake of mine own body." No wonder that those who looked on thought that GOD Himself had become his enemy.

Yet it was not so. With a tender Father's love GOD was watching all the time; and when the testing had lasted long enough to vindicate the power of GOD'S grace, and to prepare Job himself for fuller blessing, then the afflictions were taken away; and in place of the temporary trial, songs of deliverance were vouchsafed to him.

THE LOVING-KINDNESS OF THE LORD.

Nor was the blessing GOD gave to His servant a small one. During this time of affliction, which, perhaps, was not very prolonged, Job learned lessons, which all his life of prosperity had been unable to teach him. The mistakes he made in the hastiness of his spirit were corrected; his knowledge of GOD was deepened and increased; he had learned to know Him better than he could have done in any other way. He exclaimed that he had *heard of* Him previously, by the hearing of the ear, and knew GOD by hearsay only; but that now his eye *saw* Him, and that his acquaintance with GOD had become that which was the result of personal knowledge, and not of mere report. All his self-righteousness was gone: he abhorred himself in dust and ashes.

Then, when he prayed for his friends, the LORD removed the sorrow, restored to him the love and friendship of those who previously were for the time alienated, and blessed the latter end of Job more than the beginning. His sheep, his camels, his oxen, and his asses, were doubled. Again seven sons and three daughters were granted to him, and thus the number of his children also was doubled; for those who were dead were not lost, they had only gone before. And after all this, Job lived 140 years, and saw his children, and grandchildren, to the fourth generation; and finally died, being old and full of days.

May we not well say that if Job's prosperity was blessed prosperity, his adversity, likewise, was blessed adversity? "Weeping may endure for a night, but joy cometh in the morning;" and the night of weeping will bear a fruit more rich and permanent than any day of rejoicing could produce. "The evening and the morning were the first day." Light out of darkness is GOD'S order, and if sometimes our Heavenly FATHER can trust us with a trial, it is a sure presage that, if by grace the trial is accepted, He will ere long trust us with a blessing.

In this day, when material causes are so much dwelt upon that there is danger of forgetting the unseen agencies, let us not lose sight of the existence and reality of our unseen spiritual foes. Many a child of GOD knows what it is to have sore conflict with flesh and blood; and yet, as says the Apostle, "We wrestle not against flesh and blood, but against ... wicked spirits in heavenly places" (*margin*). It would be comparatively easy to deal with our visible foes, if the invisible foes were not behind them. With foes so mighty and, apart from GOD'S protecting care, so utterly irresistible, we should be helpless indeed if unprotected and unarmed.

We *need* to put on the whole armor of GOD, and to be not ignorant of Satan's devices. Let us not, on the other hand, lose sight of the precious truth that GOD alone is Almighty; that GOD is our Helper, our Protector, and our Shield, as well as our exceeding great Reward. "If God be for us, who can be against us?" Let us always be on His side, seeking to carry out His purposes; then the power of God will always be with us, and we shall be made more than conquerors through Him that loved us.

Coming to the King.

"And King Solomon gave unto the Queen of Sheba all her desire, whatsoever she asked, beside that which Solomon gave her of his royal bounty."—1 Kings x. 13.

The beautiful history recorded in the chapter from which the above words are quoted is deeply instructive to those who have learned to recognise Christ in the Scriptures. The reference to this narrative by our Lord Himself was surely designed to draw our attention to it, and gives it an added interest. The blessings, too, received by the Queen of Sheba were of no ordinary kind. She was not only pleased with her reception, and with what she saw, but all her difficulties were removed, all her petitions were granted, all her desire was fulfilled. She was satisfied—so satisfied that, with glad and thankful heart, she turned and went away to her own country to fulfil the duties which, in the providence of God, devolved upon her.

If we may learn from this narrative how to approach the Antitype of King Solomon, and to receive from Him blessings as much greater than those received by the Queen of Sheba as Christ is greater than Solomon, we shall not meditate without profit on this portion of Scripture.

In many respects we resemble the Queen of Sheba. Though of royal birth, she was doubtless, like the bride in the Song of Solomon, black, because the sun had looked upon her. The post which she was called to occupy was no easy one; in her own life, and in her duty towards others, she found many hard questions to which she saw no solution. She heard of one reigning in the power of the Lord, whose wisdom exceeded that of the wisest of men, and who, if any one could, might afford her the help that she needed. She felt sure that the reports that she heard of his wisdom and of his acts were exaggerated; yet, even allowing for this, she was prepared to take a long and difficult journey that she might see his face and prove for herself how far her difficulties could be solved by him. And she came not empty-handed; she came not only to receive, but also to give, "with a very great train, with camels that bare spices, and very much gold, and precious stones," not because she thought Solomon poor and needy, but because she knew of his magnificence she sought to bring gifts worthy of his royal dignity, and so coming she was not disappointed.

Her long journey accomplished, she reached Jerusalem, and was granted the audience with the great king which her soul craved. She not only unburdened her camels, she unburdened her own heart, and found that her difficult questions were no difficulty to him. "Solomon told her all her questions: there was not any thing hid from the king, which he told her not." And so gracious was he that, without restraint, "she communed with him of *all* that was in her heart." Surely this utter opening of the heart implies a great deal. To none but the true Solomon can we give such confidence, but to Him we may lay bare the innermost recesses of our souls, and bring the questions, difficult, perplexing, or sad, which we could breathe into no human ear.

We know what came of the questionings, in the case of the Queen of Sheba, as to whether Solomon really could be all that some enthusiasts had reported. When she had seen his wisdom, and the house that he had built, his state and his magnificence, and his ascent by which he went up into the house of the Lord, there was no more spirit in her; and she said to the king, "It was a true report that I heard in mine own land of thy acts and of thy wisdom. Howbeit I believed not the words, until I came, and mine eyes had seen it; and, behold, the half was not told me: thy wisdom and prosperity exceedeth the fame which I heard. Happy are thy men, happy are these thy servants, which stand continually before thee, and that hear thy wisdom. Blessed be the Lord thy God, which delighteth in thee, to set thee on the throne of Israel: because the Lord loved Israel for ever, therefore made He thee king, to do judgment and justice."

Was there not the true spirit of prophecy in these words? Solomon has passed away, and all his magnificence; the pleasant land is to this day desolate under the power of the Turk; but the Lord has loved Israel for ever, and soon a King shall reign in Mount Zion "before His ancients gloriously." But meanwhile this King, all unseen to human sense, is reigning, and to those who come to Him in no sordid spirit, but gladly consecrating the wealth of their heart's affection and the most worthy gifts they possess—to those who feel enriched by His acceptance of their gifts, and find pleasure in bestowing on Him for His service the best they can offer—to such there is still given the opening of heart and opening of eye to behold the King in His beauty, and to find all needed present solution of every hard question.

Do we not often give to a poor Christ rather than to a rich one? Are we not sometimes unwilling to give until we know His work to be in straits, and sometimes its very existence imperilled? Are not our hearts oft times more moved by the recital of human needs than by Christ's claim for the prosecution of the one work for which He has left His Church on earth? A famine in India, a flood in China, is more potent to bring temporal relief than the continual famine of the bread of life and of the increasing floods of heathen ungodliness. It is well, it is Christ-like, to minister temporal relief to suffering humanity, but shall the deep longings and thirstings of His soul, and the impressiveness of His last command ere He ascended on high, be less urgent? How many of the parents who refuse to let son or daughter go into the mission-field would refuse the Queen of England were she to confer the honour of a mission on their beloved children? Do we recognize the majesty of the King of Glory, and the immortal honor that appertains to His service? To those who do, the glad exclamations of the Queen of Sheba afford well-suited expressions: Happy are Thy subjects, happy are Thy servants which stand continually before Thee and hear Thy wisdom.

To the Queen of Sheba, however, more was given than to those happy subjects or to those servants who served the king in their own land. To her was given, as an eye-witness of the majesty of the king, as a glad participant of his bounty, to return to the far-off land, and to testify to those to whom, if they had heard at all, the half had not been told. Not as she came did she return, with a longing, yearning, unsatisfied heart, with duties to discharge for which she had not the wisdom;—with a royal dignity indeed, but one which brought not rest to her own spirit. Now she had *seen* the king, now *all* her desire was met; and the glorious king, after thus marvelously satisfying her, had further overwhelmed her with unthought-of gifts of his own royal bounty!

Do we know much of this, beloved friends? Has Christ become to us such a living bright reality that no post of duty shall be irksome, that as His witnesses we can return to the quiet home side, or to the distant service among the heathen, with hearts more than glad, more than satisfied; and most glad, most satisfied, when most sad and most stripped, it may be, of earthly friends and treasures? Let us put all our treasures into His hand; then He will never need to take them from us on account of heart idolatry; and if in wisdom and love He remove them for a time, He will leave no vacuum, but Himself will fill the void, Himself wipe away the tear.

There is yet more for us than it was possible to give to the Queen of Sheba. King Solomon had to send her away, he could not go with her; while, though we have to leave the conference or convention, or the early hour of holy closet communion with our Lord, for the ordinary duties of daily life, our Solomon goes with us, nay, dwells in us, to meet each fresh need and to solve each fresh perplexity as it arises. We have His word, "I will never leave thee, never fail thee, never forsake thee." Satisfied and filled to begin with, we have the Satisfier, the FILLER, with us and in us. When He says, "Whom shall We send and who will go for Us?" He means to send us on no lonely errand, but on one which will give to Him a better opportunity of revealing Himself, and to us of "finding out the greatness of His loving heart." Who will not answer Him, "Here am I, send me;" or, "Here are mine, send them"?

A Full Reward.

"It hath fully been shewed me, all that thou hast done ... and how thou hast left they father and thy mother, and the land of thy nativity, and art come unto a people which thou knewest not heretofore. The LORD recompense thy work, and a full reward be given thee of the LORD GOD of Israel, under whose wings thou art come to trust" (Ruth ii. 1 , 12).

In this interesting narrative we have another instance of the way in which the HOLY GHOST teaches by typical lives. We have dwelt on some precious lessons taught us of *our* KING by the account of the coming of the Queen of Sheba to King Solomon. There we were specially taught how our hard questions are to be solved, and our hearts to be fully satisfied. Here a still higher lesson is give us: How to serve so as to obtain "a full reward," while as to the nature of that full reward no little light is given us.

To us these lessons are of special interest, as bearing on missions to foreign nations, and perhaps they somewhat explain why He who delights to bless, and is able to bless the obedient soul, said so emphatically, "*Go*, teach all nations;" "*Go* ye into all the world." The service of GOD is a delightful privilege anywhere. Those who stay at home, however, need to become strangers and pilgrims there. This is not always easy to do in the present day; and many fail, and forget their true position. To those who are permitted to labour in foreign lands, there is a lessened danger in this respect; and hence many obtain a fuller joy in present service, and look forward to a fuller reward by-and-by, than they anticipated ere they left all for JESUS' sake.

Ruth was by nature a "stranger to the commonwealth of Israel," but by marriage with an Israelite was brought amongst that people. On the death of her husband, she still clave to her mother-in-law and to her GOD, the GOD of Israel. She so esteemed her privileged position that for it she left her native land and all its enjoyments; left parents, relatives and friends, and all those attractions that led Orpah to return to Moab. To her it was better to be the companion of her mother-in-law, poor and desolate as she was, than to enjoy for a season what in Moab might have been hers.

This sacrifice was so real that Naomi, much as she loved her daughter-in-law, and desolate as she would be without her, felt she could not wish it for her own sake merely; but when Ruth said, "*Thy* people shall by *my* people, and *thy* God *my* God," she had no further doubt to suggest, and no further obstacle to put in her way. If companionship with one of God's poor servants is so precious, what shall we say to Him who exhorts us, "Go! ... and, lo, *I* am with you"? Is He not saying: The good Shepherd must seek the wandering sheep until He find them. Go ye, too, and seek them, and in so doing you shall find My companionship ensured? Shall we decline this fellowship with Him, and leave Him, so far as we are concerned, to seek them alone?

We next find Ruth toiling in the burning sun as a gleaner, and there she meets for the first time the lord of the harvest. The beauty of the narrative of Boaz saluting his reapers with, "Thy Lord be with you," and their reply, "The Lord bless thee," must delight every reader. And poor Ruth, too though not a reaper—only a gleaner—is made most welcome, and encouraged to remain in the fields of Boaz until all the reaping is done. With touching simplicity and humility the grateful gleaner replies, "Why have *I* found grace in thine eyes, that thou shouldest take knowledge of *me*, seeing I am a stranger?" Then the lord of the harvest responds in the words we have quoted at the head of the paper, "It hath fully been showed me, all that thou hast done," etc.

Let us then turn from Boaz to the true Lord of the Harvest. Does He meet *us* there, toiling in the heat of the summer's sun? Knowing fully all *we* have done, does that knowledge bring joy to *His* heart? and is it a joy to *us* to know that He knows all? Our risen and glorious Lord, so wonderfully described in Rev. i, still walks in the midst of the golden candlesticks. Can He say to us, "I know thy works," with no word of rebuke? or do we feel the blush of shame as the eye as "a flame of fire" rests upon us? "And now, little children, abide in Him; that, when He shall appear, we may have confidence, and not be ashamed before Him at His coming."

Let us all leave the fatherland of the world, and at least become strangers and pilgrims in it. Let us all toil in some way or other in the great harvest-field, and if we may lawfully do so, let us not be slow to obey the command to "go, teach all nations." Where the need is greatest let us be found gladly obeying the Master's command. For it is *in* the harvest-field, it is among the reapers, that we shall find Him.

There is no Christian service in which faith must not be in lively exercise. At home, abroad, connected with this branch of God's work or that, without faith it is impossible to please Him. Paul may plant, Apollos water; God only gives the increase. Every true minister of God, every true missionary, every true

Sunday-school teacher and Christian worker is a faith-worker. But in the foreign field workers are peculiarly cast on G̶od̶. There are special dangers and difficulties, special weaknesses and needs that bring G̶od̶ very near— nearer than most of the workers realised Him to be while they remained at home. And to those who have gone out without human guarantee of support, who do not know when the next help may reach them, not its amount, there is an additional link with the great loving heart of our F̶ather̶ and our G̶od̶ that is unspeakably precious and welcome.

May we not say that in ever position of life when we are weak in ourselves, our friends, our circumstances, then are we strongest in Him? And when in our great needs, for ourselves or for the souls around us, we lay hold on G̶od̶ and say, "My soul, wait thou ONLY upon G̶od̶; for my expectation is from Him," what *rest* and *security* and certainty come into the waiting soul. And ah! When labouring in this spirit how words like those of our heavenly Boaz come home to the heart. "The L̶ord̶ recompense thy work, and a *full* reward be given thee of the L̶ord̶ G̶od̶ of Israel, under whose wings thou art come to trust." Happy toiler in China! Happy toiler at Home! If it is sometimes dark, the shadow is but the shadow of His wing, under which thou art abiding, under which thou art come to trust.

We will not prolong this meditation. He who comforted and blessed the lonely gleaner while the harvest lasted, became her husband when the harvest toil was past. It was *thus* the L̶ord̶ recompensed *her* work. Israel was not blessed apart from her, for David the deliverer, and Solomon the glory of Israel, were born of the seed which Boaz had through her. Soon shall come the glorious day of the espousals of C̶hrist̶ and His Church. With her He will come to deliver Israel and to judge the world and even the angels. *Ruth* little knew the honour and happiness awaiting her when she left all for G̶od̶ and His people. *We* know the purposes of G̶od̶'s grace and the glories in store for us. What manner of men, then, should we be; and how earnest and faithful in the little time which awaits us before we are called to our reward, and to meet Him in the air? When *He* says, Go! Shall we reply, No? When He asks us to continue in His harvest till the reaping is over, shall we say Him, Nay?

Under the Shepherd's Care.

A NEW YEAR'S ADDRESS.

"For ye were as sheep going astray; but are now returned unto the Shepherd

and Bishop of your souls."—1 Peter ii. 25.

"Ye were as sheep going astray." This is evidently addressed to believers. We were like sheep, blindly, willfully following an unwise leader. Not only were we following ourselves, but we in our turn have led others astray. This is true of all of us: *"All we like sheep have gone astray;"* all equally foolish, *"we have turned every one to his own way."* Our first though has been, "I like this," or "I don't like that"; never thinking what the LORD would prefer, we have just followed our own inclinations. So terribly astray were we that nothing less than the life-blood of our good SHEPHERD could atone for our sin, and save us from its power and its penalty. In Isaiah liii., we learn the substitutionary character of the death of CHRIST unmistakably, as also in the verse before our text. The GOD of the Bible is a GOD who punishes sin, and cannot pardon without atonement. The substitution of the innocent victim for the guilty offerer is so clearly taught from Genesis to Revelation, that he must be blind indeed who does not see it. Praise GOD our KINSMAN-REDEEMER has paid our debt; and "with His stripes we are healed."

II. "BUT ARE NOW RETURNED UNTO THE SHEPHERD AND BISHOP OF YOUR SOULS." Far astray as we were, by His grace we have been brought back again, and now we are "returned"—some of us scarcely returning so much as being carried to the fold by our loving SHEPHERD. And it is so blessed to realize that now we are not without a MASTER, a LEADER, a HEAD. We were intended to be followers. We always do follow; but, alas! We did not follow the right MASTER. Now the right MASTER has found us; and instead of following our own foolish lead, we *want* to follow His wise lead. And it is most restful to realize that we are not left to live a life at the mercy of circumstances, or to walk in our own wisdom. We can never foresee the future; we never fully understand the present. How dangerous would be our position were we left alone! But as believers we have been brought back; we "are now returned unto the SHEPHERD and BISHOP of our souls."

III. How blessed it is to have *such* a SHEPHERD, BISHOP, OVERSEER, One who is continually watching over us in order to provide and lead, to sustain and deliver, to meet and supply our every need! All is found in CHRIST JESUS; in His presence, in His power, in His love may we more and more rest!

I have frequently thought of words I had the privilege of hearing some years ago from Professor Charteris at a united Communion service for students in Edinburgh. He said that there had been one life on earth of steady, uninterrupted development from the cradle to the Cross; but that there had only been one such life, for the true Christian life always began where the life of CHRIST ended, *at the Cross;* and that its true development is *towards the cradle,* until the child of GOD in the child-like simplicity of faith can rest in the omnipotent arms of infinite WISDOM and LOVE. Is not this the growth and development we long for, in order that we may be among those to whom GOD will reveal the things which are hidden from the wise and prudent? The more we rest on this fact,—that we do not know the way we are going, but that we have a GUIDE who does know; that we do not know how to accomplish our service, but that He never leaves us to devise our own service;—the more restful does our life become. Then we find we have just to do this—to look to our SAVIOUR to be filled with His perfections; not to be fretting and fuming as to how the divine life shall manifest itself, but to leave the life to work spontaneously through us. A heavy bunch of grapes on a tender shoot would break it; but let the shoot abide in the vine it will grow stronger, and as the fruit develops, the strength of the branch will increase also, and the life left to its own natural and healthy development will in due time be brought to perfection

As we look forward to the months of this year, we know not where the close will find us; whether here or in the eternal Home. We know not what burdens, perplexities, or difficulties it may bring; but we know Him, whose we are, and whom we serve. HE knows all; this suffices for us.

I have been looking at a few passages which bring out the care of our LORD for His people:—

(1) 2 Tim. ii. 19, *"The foundation of GOD standeth sure, having this seal, The LORD knoweth them that are His."*—The LORD knows every one of His own. We may not know them. We may make mistakes if we judge of others. Some may be His, and we may be unaware of it. The LORD knows them that are His. This is a safe foundation. We, too, know in our souls whether the LORD is indwelling us, whether His peace fills us, sustains and blesses us.

(2) Nahum i. 7, *"The LORD is good, a stronghold in the day of trouble; and He knoweth them that trust in Him."*—He has a special knowledge of those who put their trust in Him. Though our trust at times is very poor, yet, if there be any trust at all in Him, we can say, "Help thou mine unbelief." He knows we want to trust Him better.

(3) Psalm ciii. 14, *"He knoweth our frame; He remembereth that we are dust."*—Our SHEPHERD knows our weakness. He never lays more upon us than we are able to bear.

(4) Psalm i. 6, *"The LORD knoweth the way of the righteous."*—There may be difficulties in our path; we do not foresee them, but He knows them; and when He puts forth His sheep He does not leave them to meet difficulties as best they can, but He goes before them.

(5) Job said (xxiii. 10) *"He knoweth the way that I take."*—Job did not

understand the way the LORD was leading him. He was bewildered by the LORD's dealings with him; but he had this comfort, "He knoweth the way that I take." So when we cannot understand GOD's dealings with us we may rest on the same truth.

(6) Psalm xliv. 21, *"He knoweth the secrets of the heart."*—We are often brought into circumstances of trial and misunderstanding. People imagine that this or that discipline is the fruit of this or that sin. The LORD knoweth the secrets of the heart. If we are unjustly accused or suspected, if it is asserted that we have forgotten the name of our GOD, GOD knows the secrets of our hearts. Sometimes we have trials which we cannot put into prayer; the LORD knows the secrets of our heart. There are things that affect us, and yet we cannot understand how it is that we are so affected by them. "He knoweth the secrets of the heart."

(7) 2 Peter ii. 9, *"The LORD knoweth how to deliver the godly out of temptations, and to reserve the unjust unto the day of judgment to be punished."*—Sometimes we are involved in trial because of our connection with others. GOD knew how to punish the old world and save Noah—how to punish Sodom and save Lot.

(8) Then we have many needs. We are like children, we need to be helped continually, and our SAVIOUR reminds us (Matt. vi. 8, 32) that our "heavenly FATHER knoweth what things" we "have need of"; and that if we are only concerned to seek "first the Kingdom of GOD, and His righteousness," "all these things shall be added unto" us. So that we have no need to be anxious about to-morrow. It is quite sufficient that we have a SHEPHERD, OVERSEER, FRIEND who undertakes to provide for it all.

Nay, as he told us in Psalm lxxxiv. 11, He himself is a "sun" to give us light in all times of darkness, and a "shield" to protect us in danger. The "grace" that we need for His service now, and the "glory" that shall soon crown it, are all in Him, and all for us; for, "No good thing will he withhold from them that walk uprightly." Not, from them that walk perfectly, or sinlessly—no on does that; not, from them that are blameless—though we all should be that; but if we are honestly and uprightly seeking to serve Him, no good thing will he withhold. What a rich promise this is!

IV. In conclusion: Are we all enjoying this precious truth? Are we all able to take this passage to ourselves and say, "I was a sheep going astray, but I am returned"? Can we all feel it is true for ourselves? If there be one who cannot do so, the SHEPHERD, the BISHOP, is really present, though unseen; He is here ready to receive those who will return now. "Come unto Me," is His word. If there is one burdened with sin, He is ready to pardon. If there is one burdened with care, He is present to receive your care. The LORD JESUS is waiting:

waiting to take every burden away, to accept every deposit, to fulfil every trust we confide in Him. He will be faithful to keep that which we commit to Him. We can entrust to Him the keeping of our hearts, the ordering of our lives, the care of our children, the converts whom GOD has given us, the word to which He has called us. We may trust Him to keep us, in employments in which we are brought into contact with the ungodly; yes, whatever we commit to Him, He is able to keep.

If we have come to Him, with what blessedness may we go forward into this year. We have not passed this way heretofore. We know not what burdens the LORD has for us to bear, or what blessings in store. We need not be afraid, if He gives great blessing that He will let us become puffed up; or that great difficulties will be too much for us while trusting in Him. That which was never meant for our strength will be met by His strength. May we be a docile flock, willing to be cared for by Him, and every blessing will then be ours!

Self-Denial versus Self-Assertion.

"If any man will come after Me, let him deny himself, and take up his cross daily, and follow Me.—LUKE ix. 23.

We might naturally have thought that if there was one thing in the life of the LORD JESUS CHRIST which belonged to Him alone, it was His cross-bearing. To guard against so natural a mistake, the HOLY GHOST has taken care in gospel and in epistle to draw our special attention to the oneness of the believer with CHRIST in cross-bearing; and also to prevent misunderstanding as to the character of Christian cross-bearing, and the constancy of its obligation. The LORD JESUS, in the words we are considering, teaches us that if any man, no matter who he may be, will be His disciple, he must—not *he may*—deny himself and take up his cross daily and follow his LORD.

Is there not a needs-be for this exhortation? Are not self-indulgence and self-assertion temptations to which we are ever exposed, and to which we constantly give way, without even a thought of the un-Christliness of such conduct? That we owe *something* to GOD all Christians admit; and it may be hoped that the number of those is increasing who recognise His claim to some proportionate *part* of their income. But our MASTER claims much more than a *part* of our property, of our time, of our affections. If we are saved at all, we are not our own in any sense, we are bought with a price: our bodies we must present to Him; our whole life must be for GOD.

Self-denial surely means something far greater than some slight insignificant lessening of our self-indulgences! When Peter denied CHRIST, he utterly disowned Him and disallowed His claims. In this way we are called to deny *self*, and to do it daily, if we would be CHRIST's disciples indeed. "I don't like this," or, "I do like that," must not be allowed; the only question must daily be, What would JESUS like? And His mind and will, once ascertained, must unhesitatingly be carried out.

As believers, we claim to have been crucified together with CHRIST; and Paul understood this, not merely imputatively but practically. That cross put the world to death as regards Paul, and put Paul to death as regards the world. To the Apostle nothing could have been more practical. He does not say, "I take up my cross daily," in the light, modern sense of the expression; but puts it rather as dying daily; and therefore, as one "in deaths oft," he was never surprised, or stumbled by any hardship or danger involved in his work.

We wish, however, to draw attention to another aspect of self-denial which is often overlooked, and perhaps we shall do this most intelligibly by use of the antithetical expression, self-assertion. What does the Word of GOD teach us about our rights, our claims, our dues? Does it not teach us that condemnation, banishment, eternal misery, are our own deserts? As unbelievers, we were condemned criminals; as believers, we are pardoned criminals; and whatever of good is found in us is but imparted, and to GOD alone is due the praise. Can we, then, consistently with such a position, be self-asserting and self-claimant?

It is clear that if we choose to remit a claim due to us by one who is free and our equal, that may not invalidate or affect his claim on his neighbour—no matter whether that claim be larger or smaller than the one we remitted. But what did our SAVIOUR intend to teach us by the parable of Matthew xviii. 23-35? There the King and Master and Owner of a *slave* remits His claim in clemency and pity (and does so, as our LORD elsewhere clearly shows, on express condition of His servant's forgiving as he is forgiven—Matthew vi. 14, 15); can that slave, under these circumstances, assert and claim his *rights* over his fellow?

And is not this principle of non-assertion, this aspect of self-denial, a far-reaching one? Did our LORD claim *His* rights before Pilate's bar, and assert Himself; or did His self-denial and cross-bearing go the length of waiting for His FATHER'S vindication of His character and claims? And shall *we*, in the prosecution of our work as ambassadors of Him whose kingdom is not of this world, be jealous of *our own* honour and rights, as men and as citizens of Western countries, and seek to assert the one and claim the other,—when what our MASTER wants is witness to, and reflection of, *His own* character and earthly life, and illustrations of the forbearing grace of our G<small>OD</small> and F<small>ATHER</small>?

May G<small>OD</small> work in us, and we work out in daily life, not self-*assertion* but self-*denial*—not ease and honour-seeking and right-maintaining, but right-abandoning and cross-taking—and this for the glory of His own holy Name, and for the better forwarding of His interests, whether among His own people or among the unsaved!

All Sufficiency

*"The Lord God is a Sun and Shield:
the Lord will give grace and glory:
"No good thing will He withhold from them
that walk uprightly."*
—Psalm LXXXIV. 11.

How pleasant to the heart of a true child to hear his father well spoken of, and to rejoice that he is the child of such a father. We feel that we can never thank God sufficiently for our privileged lot, who have been blessed with true and loving Christian parents. But if this be the case with regard to the dim and at best imperfect earthly reflections, what of the glorious Reality—the great Father—the source of all fatherhood, of all protection—of all that is blessed here, and true, and noble, and good—and of all the glories to which we look forward in the future? "The Lord God is a Sun and Shield: the Lord will give grace and glory: no good thing will He withhold from them that walk uprightly."

"The Lord God *is* a Sun and Shield," and this in the fullest conceivable sense. None of His works can fully reveal the great Designer, and Executor, and Upholder; and the loftiest thoughts and imaginations of the finite mind can never rise up to and comprehend the Infinite. The natural sun is inconceivably great, we cannot grasp its magnitude; it is inconceivably glorious, we cannot bear to gaze for one moment on its untempered light. The source to us of all heat, we have to shield ourselves from its tropical power, though millions of miles from its surface: the sustainer of the essential conditions of physical life, and the great ruler and centre of the solar system
—how great and glorious is the natural sun! And yet it may be the very smallest of all the countless suns that God has made! What of the glorious Maker of them all!

"The Lord God *is* a Sun." Ah! He deserves the name, He *is* the Reality of all that sun or suns exhibit or suggest. My reader, is he *the* Sun to *you*? Do you count *all* that to be darkness which does not come form and accord with His light: *all* that to be disorder which does not implicitly accept and delight in His rule? "O Lord of Hosts, blessed is the man that trusteth to Thee!" Self- will is unmingled folly, and can only end in injury and loss.

And the Lord God *is* a Shield. Dangers encompass us, unseen at every moment. Within us, in the wonderful and delicate organisation of our bodies
—around us, when in circumstances of the greatest comfort and apparent

safety—are dangers unseen, which at any moment might terminate our earthly career. Dangers *seen* sometimes appal us, or appal those who love us: but they are not more real than many we never dream of. Why do we live so safely, then? Because the Lord God *is* a Shield.

Foes, too, are never far from us. The world, the flesh, and the devil are very real; and unaided we have no power to keep or deliver ourselves from them. But the Lord God *is* a Shield. It is a small matter then to go to China, a very small additional risk to run; for there, as here, the Lord God *is* a Shield. Should war break out, in this we may be confident; for He has said He will never fail nor forsake His own. Only when our work is done will He take us home; and this He will do whether we serve Him here or there. To *know* and to *do* His will—this is our safety; this is our rest.

Sweet are his promises—grace will He give, and glory. Grace all unmerited and free—that which is really for our good, for Christ's deservings, not for ours. And glory too—glory now, the glory of *being* His, of *serving* Him in each least duty of life, and glory in the soul. Glory apparent, too, as with unveiled faces we behold and rejoice in His glory, and reflect it ever more and more. And glory to come, when we have done and suffered His will here, and are "for ever with the Lord!"

"No *good* thing will He withhold from them that walk uprightly." Ah! How often, when we have been dissatisfied with the ways of God, we ought to have been dissatisfied with our own ways! We did not think, perhaps, that in some matter or other we were not walking uprightly. If not so, however, then the thing we desired was *not* for our good, and therefore was not given; or the thing we feared was essential to our good, and hence was not withheld. We are often mistaken: God, never. "No *good* thing will He withhold": shall we be so foolish, so wayward, as after this to *desire* that which our Father in heaven withholds?

But sweet as are God's promises, the Promiser is greater and better. Finite human words fetter the expression of the heart of the Infinite Giver. Hence if we had claimed all the promises, had opened our mouths most wide, and had asked with all the blessed presumption of loved and favoured children—yet, above and beyond the promises, He would still be able to do exceeding abundantly *above* all we ask or think. He delights to do so! Let not low thoughts, God-dishonouring thoughts, unbelieving, distrustful thoughts, limit His blessings; for "*No* good thing will He withhold from them that walk uprightly."